MONSTER HUNTERS

hunt the ozark howler

by Jan Fields

Illustrated by Scott Brundage

An Imprint of Magic Wagon
abdopublishing.com

abdopublishing.com

Published by Magic Wagon, a division of ABDO, PO Box 398166, Minneapolis, Minnesota 55439. Copyright © 2017 by Abdo Consulting Group, Inc. International copyrights reserved in all countries. No part of this book may be reproduced in any form without written permission from the publisher. Calico™ is a trademark and logo of Magic Wagon.

Printed in the United States of America, North Mankato, Minnesota.
052016
092016

Written by Jan Fields
Illustrated by Scott Brundage
Edited by Tamara L. Britton & Megan M. Gunderson
Design Contributors: Candice Keimig & Laura Mitchell

Library of Congress Cataloging-in-Publication Data

Names: Fields, Jan, author. | Brundage, Scott, illustrator. | Fields, Jan. Monster hunters.
Title: Hunt the Ozark howler / by Jan Fields ; illustrated by Scott Brundage.
Description: Minneapolis, MN : Magic Wagon, [2017] | Series: Monster hunters
| Summary: When the Discover Cryptids crew arrives in Arkansas to investigate the Ozark Howler, possibly an escaped exotic big cat, they find themselves in direct competition with a rival television crew for the program Bump in the Night--but when they are examining signs of the monster Gabe falls into the river and is swept away.
Identifiers: LCCN 2016016971 | ISBN 9781624021527 (lib. bdg.) | ISBN 9781680779820 (ebook)
Subjects: LCSH: Monsters--Juvenile fiction. | Exotic animals--Juvenile fiction. | Video recording--Juvenile fiction. | Action photography--Juvenile fiction. | Adventure stories. | Ozark Mountains--Juvenile fiction. | Arkansas--Juvenile fiction. | CYAC: Monsters--Fiction. | Animals--Fiction. | Cat family (Mammals)--Fiction. | Video recording--Fiction. | Photography--Fiction. | Adventure and adventurers--Fiction. | Ozark Mountains--Fiction. | Arkansas--Fiction.
Classification: LCC PZ7.F479177 Hw 2016 | DDC 813.6 [Fic] --dc23
LC record available at https://lccn.loc.gov/2016016971

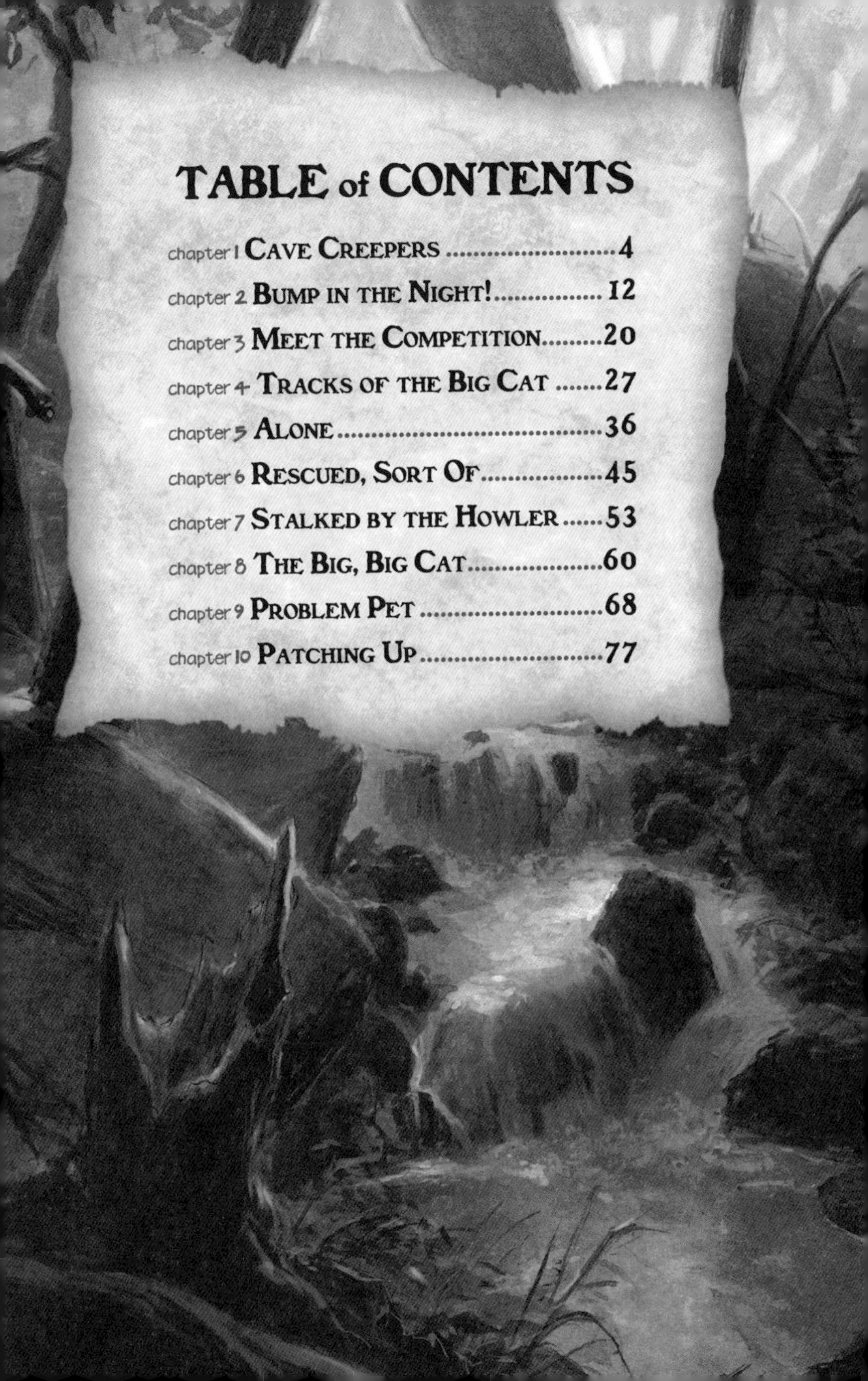

TABLE of CONTENTS

chapter 1

Cave Creepers

Darkness inside a cave is different from the darkness outside. Outside, the moon may brighten the world to a pale gray shadow. Outside, the spilled glitter of stars sparkle against the black velvet sky. Outside, you might look into the distance at the light pollution seeping from a town or city.

In a cave, you see nothing. No stars. No shadows. Just darkness so deep it presses against your skin.

Gabe Brown didn't usually think much about the dark. As part of the team chasing monsters all over America for his brother's web show, *Discover Cryptids*, Gabe had seen a lot of darkness. Cryptids like dark nights, dark water,

and dark shadows. Gabe thought he was done being scared of the dark. He was wrong.

His best friend Tyler stomped the back of Gabe's boots, again. "Could you maybe give me a little room?" Gabe asked, as he shrugged his friend off.

Tyler took a half step back but kept a hand on Gabe's backpack. "No, you have the flashlight. I'd walk on top of you if I could."

"I thought that's what you were doing. Do you want the light?" Gabe asked, not that he wanted to give it up.

"And be in the lead?" Tyler yelped. "No. I figure the killer reptoid will go after the guy with the light."

"Then shouldn't you back up out of slashing range?" Gabe asked.

Tyler thought for a moment, then shook his head. "In nature films, the predators always go after the straggler. I'm not straggling."

"You could straggle a little," Gabe muttered. The beam of the flashlight lit the uneven cave floor ahead, but it was growing dimmer. So far, Tyler hadn't noticed, but Gabe could see the darkness gobbling up more and more of their small light.

Gabe cleared his throat. "Do you have any batteries in your backpack?"

"No. I have a water bottle, two comic books, five granola bars, and an umbrella."

Gabe stopped in his tracks and turned to look at his friend. "An umbrella? We're in a cave."

"I always carry an umbrella," Tyler said. "Remember when we were almost eaten by a bear? We were saved by an umbrella. I don't leave the van without one."

"I really don't think we're going to be attacked by a bear in here."

"Hey, something was growling," Tyler said,

his gaze darting toward the darkness around them.

It felt like hours since they heard the last growl. That growl had sent Tyler running away from the group. Gabe ran after him, but when Tyler was scared, he was fast. Gabe didn't catch up to him until Tyler tripped over a rock. The fall broke his flashlight. Now they had one flashlight and a whole lot of empty cave passages between them and their friends.

On top of that, they couldn't find the broken flashlight. Gabe wished they'd looked harder. They could have used the batteries. He knew his brother Ben and their friend Sean must be looking for them, but the cave was a maze. That's why Ben had insisted they stick together in the first place.

With a sigh, Gabe admitted, "The flashlight is getting dimmer. My batteries are running down."

"You mean we're going to be in the dark?"

Tyler's eyes widened and he began yelling. "Help! Someone help!" His screams echoed off the walls of the cave.

Gabe put his hand over Tyler's mouth. "We already tried yelling."

"I'm turning off the light," Gabe said. "I don't think we're getting anywhere. If we were going in the right direction, we would have come to the entrance by now."

Both boys fell silent for a moment. In the total stillness, they heard a scuffling sound. Tyler's face lit up. "They found us! Hey, we're over here!"

Something about the odd rustling made the hair on the back of Gabe's neck stand up. He caught Tyler's arm. "Hold on," he whispered. "I don't think that's Ben."

"Of course it is," Tyler said, pulling away. "Ben! Sean!"

"Listen!" Gabe hissed.

Tyler fell silent. They heard odd breathy

snorts. "That isn't Ben," Gabe whispered. He pulled Tyler backward away from the sounds. A low, deep growl replaced the snorts.

Behind them, the snorting and growls grew louder. The boys ran then, as fast as they dared to in the shadowy cave.

Then Gabe saw that the ground ahead of them looked dark, too dark. "Wait," he said, pulling Tyler, who would have run ahead. "I think that's a hole." They crept close. It was a deep chasm that stretched across the whole passage. There was no way around it.

"Maybe we can jump over it," Tyler suggested.

Gabe shone his feeble flash beam, but it didn't reach the other side. "I can't tell how wide it is."

Behind them, the snorting and growling sounded closer.

"We have to do something!" Tyler said.

Gabe looked around, flashing the weak beam into a deep crack in the wall of the

passage. He hurried over to it, shining the beam in, hoping it was a side tunnel. It wasn't. The flashlight picked up a dead end only a few feet in. Still, it might give them someplace to hide.

"In here," he said to Tyler. As his friend passed, Gabe pulled open Tyler's backpack and took out the umbrella.

"I don't think it's going to rain in there," Tyler whispered.

Gabe didn't answer, he just pushed Tyler to the far wall. "Crouch down," he whispered. The boys wedged as close to the ground possible, and Gabe opened the umbrella in front of them and turned off the light.

The shuffling, snorting sounds grew louder and Gabe could feel Tyler shaking beside him. He couldn't see anything at all in the complete darkness of the cave. Gabe held his breath as whatever moved through the darkness grew close and sniffed. A low growl vibrated through the umbrella handle.

Gabe closed his eyes and waited for the attack to begin.

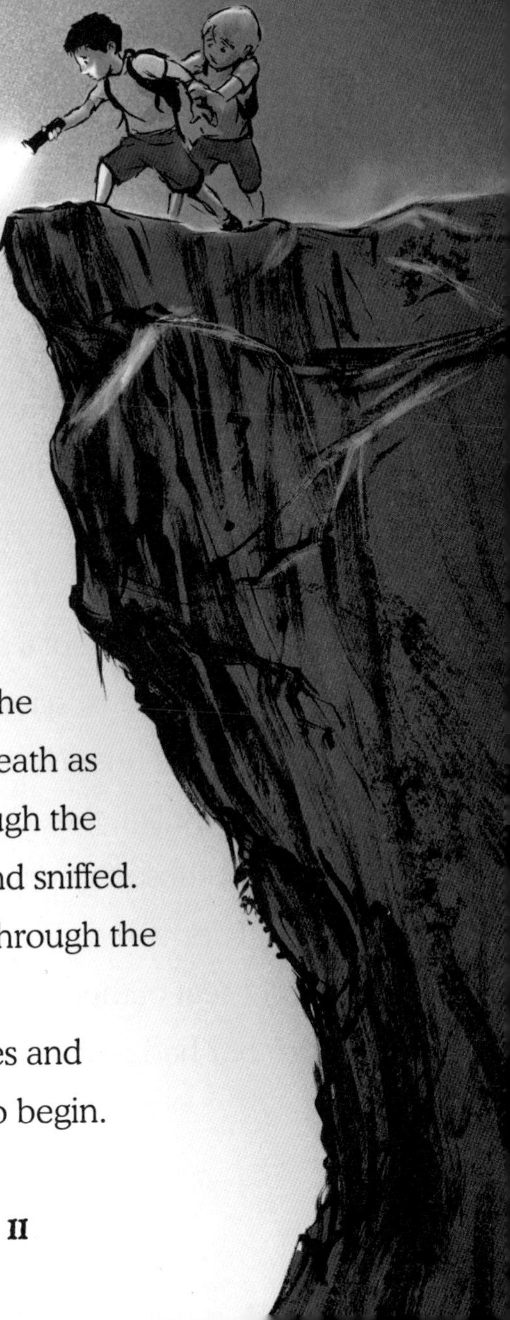

chapter 2

BUMP IN THE NIGHT!

The tour bus parked in the hotel lot couldn't have been any flashier. Gabe doubted the small northern Arkansas town deep in the Ozark Mountains saw buses like that one very often.

Red dripping letters spelled out "Bump in the Night" on the midnight blue bus. *Bump in the Night* was the name of a popular cable television show about ghosts, aliens, and monsters. Near the back of the bus, a huge face grinned at them. It was Ace Rollin, the show's host.

"Aren't those the guys who hired all of your crew?" Tyler asked. For once, he was riding in the front seat of their small van. Gabe suspected his brother had regretted that seating plan miles ago.

Ben spoke between clenched teeth. "Yes."

Tyler didn't seem to notice Ben's tension as he bounced in his seat. "Why are they here?"

"They're looking for the Ozark Howler," Sean suggested. "Same as us."

"It doesn't matter," Ben said. He wrenched the wheel sharply, nearly throwing them into the nearest parking space. "I'll go check in, then I have to call my contact at Wild Hope." He was out of the van and slamming the door before anyone could speak.

Wild Hope was an organization dedicated to stopping the trade in exotic animals as pets. The people at Wild Hope believed the Ozark Howler was really an escaped pet. Gabe hoped the Howler wasn't a pet. He wanted the Monster Hunters to find evidence of real cryptids, mystery creatures, not just lost pets.

"That bus is so cool," Tyler said, jerking Gabe out of his musing. "Do you think Ace Rollin is

actually in there? Maybe we could work together. We could be on television!"

"Don't let Ben hear you say that," Gabe said. "He'll be sorry he got us out of that cave in Tennessee."

Tyler crossed his arms. "We would have gotten out on our own after a while."

"You were hiding," Sean said. "Behind an umbrella. From a dog."

"We didn't know it was a dog," Tyler said. "It was dark."

Sean continued to talk as if Tyler hadn't said anything. "A little bitty bulldog."

"It didn't sound little," Tyler insisted. "Those caves echo. And the dog's owner gave us a reward for bringing it out. We were heroes."

"Heroes hiding behind an umbrella."

Tyler turned around in his seat to look out the front window. "Let's go out and look at that bus. Wouldn't it be cool if we had a bus like that?"

"There's nothing about that bus that we need," Gabe answered, slumping down in his seat. He folded his arms over his chest.

"Look at it this way," Tyler said. "If Mr. Rollin didn't steal away all the crew of *Discover Cryptids* from Ben, we'd still be stuck at home. Right? We should like him."

Gabe wouldn't go that far. But he had to admit that Tyler had a point. He looked out the window. He had to admit the bus was cool. "Okay. Let's go look at it."

The bus was even more impressive up close. It didn't have any of the dents, scratches, or dirt that covered the *Discover Cryptids* van. Their van didn't even have a cool sign. Gabe stuffed his hands in the pockets of his shorts. "The bus is nice. But I like the van."

"I bet this thing has a kitchen or at least a fridge," Tyler said. He turned to look at them wide-eyed. "Maybe even a TV!"

"It has a TV and a fridge."

The boys turned to face a man about Ben's age with curly blond hair and a beard. As he saw their faces, his lit up. "Gabe? Is that you?"

Gabe frowned slightly. "Hi, Orson."

Orson strode over and wrapped Gabe in a hug. "It's great to see you, kid. You're taller." He held Gabe out at arm's length. "Definitely taller."

Gabe didn't know what to do. Orson Haas had been his brother's best friend since they were kids. When Orson left *Discover Cryptids* to work for the cable network, it hurt Ben a lot.

Luckily Orson let go of Gabe and turned to Sean and Tyler. "So this must be the rest of the team. I've seen the show. You guys are doing great work."

"No thanks to you," Gabe said.

Orson gave him a hurt glance. "I made a decision to advance my career. It had nothing to do with my feelings about you or Ben."

"That much was clear," Gabe answered. "You definitely weren't concerned about feelings."

"Don't be like that," Orson said, clapping Gabe on the back. "I'm glad to see you. And glad to meet the new team."

"Do you think we could see inside the bus?" Tyler asked.

Orson gave Tyler a grin. "I think that can be arranged."

Before Gabe could answer, he saw Ben storming toward them. "What are you guys doing over here?" he asked.

"We wanted a closer look at the bus," Tyler said.

"Benjamin!" Orson said, the grin spreading across his face again as he took a step toward Ben. "It's good to see you, man."

Ben's expression stopped him in his tracks. "Orson," Ben said with a short nod. "I see you're still working for Rollin."

Orson shook his head. "I don't work for Rollin. I work for the cable network. You could be working there too."

Ben snorted. "I've seen that show. It's full of big talk and no honest answers. I think I'll pass."

Orson shrugged. "People don't really want us to debunk monsters. They want us to give them permission to believe."

"No," Ben said. "I think people want us to be honest about the real cryptids and the hoaxes."

Orson looked at his old friend sadly "And

that's why your show is on the Internet, and ours is on a major cable channel."

Tyler and Sean winced, but Ben didn't even flinch. "So what does *Bump in the Night* hope to do?" Ben asked. "Convince people there really is a giant panther with horns roaming the mountains?"

Orson smiled. "Why not? This time we have proof. The Ozark Howler is real!"

chapter 3

Meet the Competition

Sean looked at Orson with interest. "You have evidence of a giant creature that is half bear and half cat? I've seen evidence about this creature before, and it was a hoax."

Orson kept his wide grin. "Not this time. This time there's real proof."

Ben crossed his arms over his chest and leaned against the side of the bus. "Really? What kind of proof?"

"A video shot in Miller's Crossing." At Ben's skeptical snort, Orson added, "I've seen it. It looks real and scary. That cat is big, really big. Lion big."

"Wildlife officials believe reports of large wild felines in the Ozark Mountains are the result

of escaped exotic pets," Sean said. "Perhaps someone captured one on video, unless the creature in the video has bear-like qualities."

Orson shuddered. "I can't imagine anyone keeping something like that for a pet. Have you read the reports of glowing eyes?"

"I've read all the reports," Sean said.

"Well, the beast in the video had glowing eyes."

Sean launched into facts mode. "The eyes of many nocturnal animal seem to glow on camera. They have special reflective cells in their eyes to make the best use of available light to see. These cells make their eyes appear to glow."

Orson grunted. "I don't know about all that, professor, but that monster had glowing eyes."

"Did it have horns?" Sean asked. "Some reports say the Ozark Howler has horns like a sheep. I feel that is an unlikely addition to the mythology."

Orson stared at Sean for a moment. "I didn't see any horns, but it was dark in the video. Still, it was clearly a huge cat."

"Assuming you weren't fooled by a hoax," Ben said. "It's happened to *Bump in the Night* before."

"Guys," Tyler said. "Guys, look."

Gabe looked in the direction Tyler pointed. At the end of the bus, a man stood with his hands on his hips and his head turned to show off his good side. His wide smile revealed perfect teeth. It was Ace Rollin. Gabe almost groaned.

The cable host finished posing and strode toward them. "Do I hear you talking about our

newest investigation with some young fans?"

"These guys are the crew of *Discover Cryptids*," Orson said.

Ace turned a vague smile toward them. "Oh, is that a new children's show?"

"No," Orson said. "It's the Internet show you were watching last week."

The cable host's cheeks reddened, but he just waved a hand. "I do so much research, it's hard to keep track of every little website."

"If you research so much, you must know the history of Internet hoaxes that surround the Ozark Howler," Ben said, crossing his arms over his chest and glaring at the host.

Ace narrowed his eyes. "Yes, I know about past hoaxes. But we have the video that my associate is doing such a poor job of keeping secret. It's no hoax."

"I didn't see any reason to keep it secret," Orson said. "We're all after the truth."

"We're after ratings," Ace said. "So we don't share with the competition."

"So now we're the competition?" Ben said, his frown sliding into a smile. "I thought we were a kiddie show that you knew nothing about."

Before Ace could respond to that, a lanky guy in a *Bump in the Night* T-shirt leaned around the end of the bus. "Guys, we need to get going. I just saw a new post on the *Bump* discussion boards. Someone just saw the Howler in the Miller's Crossing woods." The guy paused, then blurted. "And it's leaving physical evidence all over the place."

"Time to make some TV," Ace said. He turned a quick smile in the direction of Ben. "Nice to meet you boys. Be sure to catch *Bump in the Night*. We'll show you how to hunt monsters."

Orson gave them an apologetic smile and a shrug before following Ace around the bus and out of sight.

"I guess that means we don't get to see inside the bus," Tyler said.

Ben put out his hands and herded them toward the van. "Get in the van. We can easily outrun that parade float to Miller's Crossing."

"I thought we were meeting your contact about exotic pets," Gabe said.

"I'll call her and reschedule," Ben insisted.

They jumped into the van. The boys hurried to buckle in, as Ben raced out of the parking lot. He tossed his phone over his shoulder to Gabe. "Give Dr. Iverson a call. She's in my contacts. Tell her we can't make the meeting and why."

Ben yelled more orders from the front seat. "Sean, find those posts about the Howler. I know where Miller's Crossing is, but we need to know exactly where the creature has been spotted."

Clearly Ben was determined to meet the challenge that Ace Rollin had thrown down. Gabe just hoped they survived it.

chapter 4

Tracks of the Big Cat

Miller's Crossing turned out to be little more than a bend in the road. A lone gas station with a gravel parking lot was the only business. The van swung into the lot where only a battered pick-up truck and a single car were parked.

"We beat them!" Tyler whooped.

"Are you sure this is the spot?" Ben asked, twisting in his seat to look at Sean.

Sean didn't even look up from his tablet. "According to posts I found, the monster cat was behind this building."

"That's enough for me," Ben said. "Grab the gear."

Gabe snatched up the camera, while Tyler went after the sound equipment. As usual, Sean

considered his computer tablet to be all the gear he needed to carry. They piled out of the van and ran after Ben.

"Hey!" The group turned at the sound of the shout. Just outside the front door of the building, an older man with a long, thick beard pointed at them. "Where do you kids think you're going?"

"We're with *Discover Cryptids*," Ben said, stepping between Gabe and Tyler. "We're here because of the post about the big cat."

The man narrowed his eyes. "Why'd they send kids out to investigate?"

"This is my team," Ben said. "I can assure you that we're experienced in this sort of thing. Are you the one who spotted the cat?"

The man nodded. "I saw it out the bathroom window. You don't want to take kids back there. I wouldn't go back there myself. That ain't no house cat."

"You said it left evidence?" Sean asked.

The old man looked at Sean for a long moment, then said. "It pooped. And it scratched that big old oak that's right at the edge of the woods there, near the creek."

Sean's face brightened. "We could get a sample of scat for analyzing."

Gabe wrinkled his nose. He remembered what scat meant. "I'm not scooping up lion poop."

Tyler waved a hand under his nose. "Me either."

"Don't worry about the poop now," Ben said. "Let's go check out the area."

"You watch those kids," the man said, pointing at Ben. "That Howler is dangerous. It'll eat up a kid as soon as look at him."

"Let me worry about that," Ben said. Clearly done with the conversation, he turned and trotted toward the rear of the building.

Gabe slung an arm around Tyler's shoulders.

"Look on the bright side. If we see the Howler, we'll run. Then all you have to do is run faster than Sean."

Tyler's face brightened. "Yeah, I hadn't thought of it that way. I can outrun Sean."

Sean frowned at his friends. "I hardly see why that would be the bright side."

"It is if you're me!" Tyler said, thumping his friend on the back.

The old man shouted after them, "You boys be careful. We've had a lot of rain. That creek is rough as a river."

"Sure, sure," Tyler yelled over his shoulder as the boys trotted to catch up with Ben. When they rounded the corner of the building, Gabe held up the camera. He began shooting immediately in case the Ozark Howler was still there. An open space lay between the back of the gas station and the edge of the woods. The clearing was covered with rock, scrub grass, and scattered

trash. There was no sign of a giant black cat.

Ben crossed the clearing and stopped next to one of the twisted trees. "Come and get a shot of this," he called back to Gabe.

Slowly the tree became clearer in the viewfinder. Gabe saw deep scratches in the bark. He lowered the camera and touched them. "Do you think the Howler made these?"

"It could have been a bear," Sean said. Gabe turned to see his friend squatting beside a pile of poop. "According to the National Park Service, black bear sightings are rare but they have been known to scratch trees."

Everyone turned at the deep rumble of a large diesel engine pulling off the road. "Great," Ben grumbled.

Gabe watched the end of the building, waiting for the others to come around. "We're all trying to do the same thing. Maybe we could work together," he said.

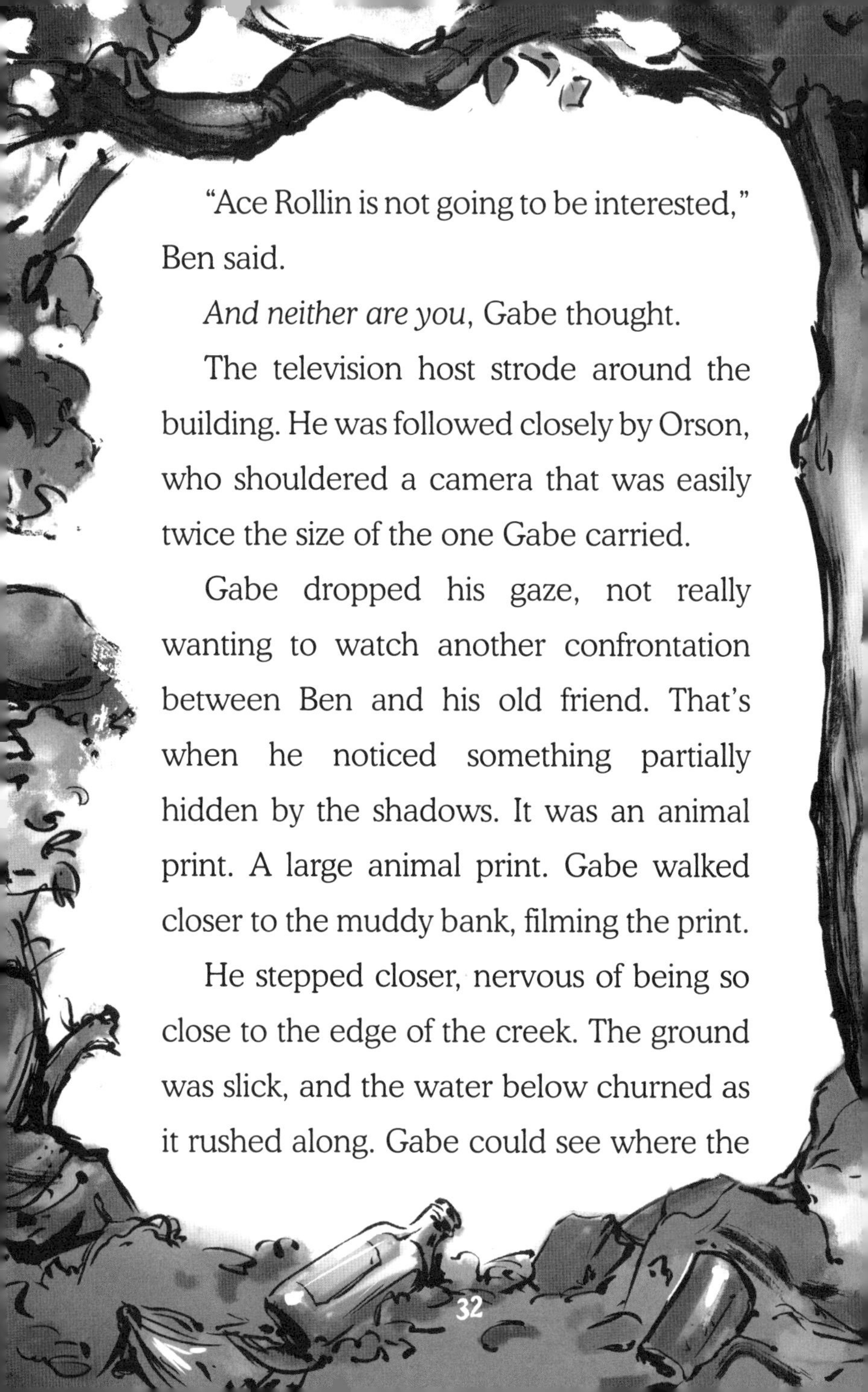

"Ace Rollin is not going to be interested," Ben said.

And neither are you, Gabe thought.

The television host strode around the building. He was followed closely by Orson, who shouldered a camera that was easily twice the size of the one Gabe carried.

Gabe dropped his gaze, not really wanting to watch another confrontation between Ben and his old friend. That's when he noticed something partially hidden by the shadows. It was an animal print. A large animal print. Gabe walked closer to the muddy bank, filming the print.

He stepped closer, nervous of being so close to the edge of the creek. The ground was slick, and the water below churned as it rushed along. Gabe could see where the

swollen creek had begun to undercut the bank.

He turned his attention away from the water and focused on the track. The print was wide and deep. Gabe couldn't tell if it was from a bear or a big cat. Sean would know. Could he signal Sean without drawing too much attention?

He really didn't need to worry. Everyone's eyes were on Ben and Ace Rollin. The two stood nose to nose over the pile of poop. "We were here first," Ben insisted. "So back off."

"We have far better facilities to analyze the evidence," Ace said with a smug smile. "Aren't you the one who said the most important thing was getting at the truth?"

"You wouldn't know the truth if it bit you!" Ben growled.

"Hey," Tyler shouted and both of the men looked at him. "You guys do understand that you're arguing over who owns poop, right?"

Gabe tuned out the arguing and began

carefully circling the track. He wanted the best angle so the light made the track clear. Then he heard Ace Rollin's voice, "Hey, kid, what are you looking at over there? Orson, get that shot!"

Orson rushed toward Gabe. Without thinking, Gabe took a step back and slipped on the muddy bank. He clutched his camera close to protect it in case he fell, but he was in much worse trouble than that. His slip put him on a section of undercut bank. It crumbled. Gabe plunged into the rushing water below.

chapter 5

Alone

Though he'd always been a strong swimmer, Gabe could do little against the rushing water as it carried him downstream. Again and again, he slammed into a rock or sunken log. More than once, he was dragged under, only to pop to the surface in seconds, coughing and gasping.

He had to get out of the river. If he hit a rock too hard, it could knock him out. If that happened, he would drown. Gabe knew he couldn't swim directly across the wide creek. The current was too strong. Instead he slowly angled toward the bank as he rushed downstream.

It was tough to stay pointed in the direction he needed. The cold and the battering left his legs numb. More than once, the current spun

him in circles. But Gabe didn't panic. He had to get to shore. Ben would be looking for him.

After what seemed like forever, Gabe saw a tree capsized into the water. The roots still lay on the shore. If he could catch hold of it, he might finally get out.

Gabe clutched the camera tightly. He didn't know if it was already destroyed, but he wasn't giving it up now. He shoved it under his shirt to free his hands. Then when the creek raced under the fallen tree, Gabe raised his arms high.

When he slammed into the fallen tree, the pain was terrible. He thought for a moment that he'd broken his arm. He gently flexed his elbow and shoulder. He could move. So he did.

Gabe inched toward the shore, using branches from the tree like a sideways ladder. It was slow going. But finally he stretched his arm and grabbed a sapling rooted in the creek bank. He dragged himself up onto the muddy ground.

He lay on his back in the mud, panting. Gabe had been in trouble before since he joined Ben hunting cryptids. He'd gotten lost in the woods, lost in a cave, locked up by bad guys, and stuck in a sewer. Usually Tyler was with him. In fact, Tyler normally got them into the trouble in the first place. "This one is all mine, buddy," he said.

Gabe sat up carefully. The feeling was returning to his legs. He liked the numbness a

lot better. But his arm was still sore. He felt like someone had been beating him with a big stick.

Using a tree to help him to his feet, Gabe looked around. The woods were thick. All he heard was the roar of the creek beside him. How far had the creek carried him from the store?

"Hey!" he yelled. "Can anyone hear me?" Gabe listened closely but no one answered.

He pulled his cell phone out of his hip pocket. The screen was shattered. No amount of button

pushing woke the thing up. Happily, the camera appeared to be in much better shape. The view screen lit up instantly when he turned it on. Too bad he couldn't call for help with it.

Gabe scanned the woods with the camera, not knowing what good the footage would do. It just seemed easier to think with a camera in his hand.

If he followed the creek back upstream, he had to reach the grocery, sooner or later. He shivered. Sooner would be good. The water in the creek was freezing, and he wasn't warming up much in the shadowy woods.

Though he had to scramble over a couple young trees that had fallen in the recent storms, the walk wasn't too tough at first. Walking made him feel warmer and loosened his sore muscles.

Soon though, the thick brush pushed him away from the edge of the bank. With the sound of the creek in his right ear, he could keep going

in the right direction. More and more, he had to walk around the larger obstructions.

As Gabe got farther from the rushing creek, he could hear other sounds. The woods rustled and snapped. Sometimes he spotted a squirrel rummaging under a tree or a bird fluttering through a tangle of underbrush. Sometimes he had no idea what lurked outside his vision. That's when his imagination filled in the blanks in the scariest way possible.

"I bet Sean knows how many people are eaten by big cats every year," Gabe said. "He'd tell me without even being asked." He stopped at a particularly loud rustle up ahead. "I'm so glad Sean isn't here."

Gabe stepped back away from the sound. Sometimes a noise from a squirrel or a deer was really loud. "Are you a deer?" he whispered.

Whatever the creature was, it didn't answer Gabe's quiet question. A pair of old maple trees

had grown together into a wide, twisted trunk. Gabe stepped behind them. The noise stopped. He waited. Standing so still, he could feel the chill from his wet clothes again, making him shiver.

Gabe couldn't stand around in the woods until he froze. He needed to get back to his friends. He crept around the wide tree trunk, then walked slowly toward the shadows ahead. He turned on the camera, using the camera's light to brighten the way ahead.

That's when he saw it.

A paw print marked the muddy ground ahead. Gabe wished he knew the difference between a cat track and a bear track. Of course, if it was the Ozark Howler's track, it was both cat and bear according to the legends. He held out his hand. It looked tiny next to the giant print.

He stood still, the camera's light shining on the print. What should he do? If he walked on,

he might run smack into whatever had made that track. He'd already heard it. If he walked in any other direction, he would end up hopelessly lost. If he sat down and waited for rescue, he'd freeze.

"Lots of choices," he said. "All bad."

Gabe turned off the light on the camera to conserve the battery. He might need it if he were still in the woods when it got dark. Surely his brother would find him before then. They had to be looking for him, right?

He thought of Ben's argument with Ace Rollin. Would his brother let Rollin take over that scene where all the evidence lay? "Of course he would," Gabe said, wishing his voice sounded surer. "He's my brother."

He squared his shoulders and marched forward. He'd get back to the store. He'd help collect the evidence. He would not get eaten. He had decided. That's when he heard the loudest

rustling yet in the brush ahead. He turned on the camera again.

At some point in the past, two trees had fallen, slamming into one another before they could reach the ground. They'd created a cave of branches that were now partially overgrown with what looked like blackberry briars. Seeing the briars made him remember one of Sean's fun facts about the Ozark Mountains. They had abundant fruit-growing areas.

Unfortunately, it wasn't blackberries making the noises he heard. Inside that snarled mess, the rustling grew louder still. Something was coming through the deadfall straight at him. Something big!

chapter 6

Rescued, Sort Of

Gabe jumped back, tripping over a root near his feet and falling on his rear. He crab walked backward, shrieking all the while. Then something burst through the brush into the clearing. It wasn't a cat or a bear. It was Ben. He looked as wet and rough as Gabe.

"What are you screaming about?" Ben yelled.

Gabe closed his mouth with a snap. "No reason." Then he grinned up at his brother. "You came after me."

"Of course I came after you." Ben reached down and took his hand, hauling him to his feet. "You're my little brother."

"I know," Gabe said. "But won't Ace Rollin get the scoop at the store?"

Ben stared at Gabe. "Did you hit your head? I don't care about that. You fell in the river."

"The man at the store said it was a creek," Gabe answered.

"It felt like a river to me, especially when I slammed into a few rocks."

Gabe looked at his brother's muddy, wet clothes. "You fell in too?"

"No. I jumped in to save you. The water was a little rougher than I expected. I thought I caught sight of you once. I spotted a flash of color in the trees. I managed to climb out of the creek there, but I found someone's trash. By then I really didn't want to be in the creek anymore. I thought I'd try looking for you overland." He shrugged. "And here we are."

"I'm glad you're here," Gabe said, his voice beginning to shake as the cold sunk deeper into him. "We should walk. That's how I've been staying warm."

Ben leaned closer to his brother. "Not very warm. Your lips are blue." He took hold of Gabe's arm. "You're freezing. We have to get these wet clothes dry."

"Can't we just go back to the store?" Gabe asked, his voice stuttering as he shook harder.

"That's miles away," his brother answered. "You're not going to be able to manage unless we get you warmed up."

Gabe wanted to tell his brother about the animal tracks he'd seen. But he couldn't explain clearly with his teeth chattering. "W-w-warm up, h-h-how?" he asked.

"A fire of course," Ben said. He looked around the woods. "Come on. We'll find a clearing near the water and build it there. The smoke will help if anyone is looking for us."

Gabe nodded. As they walked, he picked up dead sticks for the fire, though his fingers seemed unusually clumsy. Finally, they found a

spot near the water. "I'll start the fire," Ben said. "Take off your clothes."

"What?" Gabe yelped. If the Ozark Howler burst out of the woods to eat them, he'd really rather not meet it with no clothes on.

"They won't dry fast enough on you," Ben said. "We can hang our clothes around us from these branches. The fire will dry them."

It sounded sensible. While Ben set fire to his small pile of kindling, Gabe peeled off his T-shirt and shorts. Then he kicked off his sneakers and hung his socks on a branch. He danced around in the cold air, hugging his chest.

"I'm almost there," Ben said. He puffed on the tiny fire. The kindling quickly burst into flame and Ben fed the tiny fire with more dry sticks, adding bigger and bigger sticks until it was burning well.

"I am in love with this fire," Gabe said as he bent close to the warm fire.

"Sorry," Ben said as he shucked off his clothes. "I can't leave you two alone." He hung his wet things up on branches as Gabe had done.

Gabe thrust his hands toward the fire. "Do you think anyone will come looking for us?"

Ben shook his head and frowned. "You mean the guys from *Bump in the Night*? That doesn't seem likely."

"Are you going to stay mad at Orson forever?" Gabe asked. "Because I think he feels bad."

Ben poked another stick into the fire. "He should."

"Is it really that terrible?" Gabe asked quietly. "Working with the guys and me?"

Ben's attention jerked to Gabe. "Of course not." Before he could say anything else, they heard thrashing in the bushes. Ben smiled. "Hey, maybe they found us after all."

Gabe shifted, sharply aware again that he was sitting in his underwear. "Or maybe the

Howler did."

Before Ben could respond, a deer crashed out of the brush and into the clearing. It took one look at Ben and Gabe, then leaped away into the brush on the other side of the clearing.

"Or, it might just be a deer," Ben said.

Gabe looked around. He wondered if something had chased the deer into the clearing. "I saw some big tracks before, right there where you found me. I don't know if it was a cat or a bear or an Ozark Howler."

Ben stood up. "Can you show me the tracks?"

"Can I put my clothes back on first?"

Ben laughed. "Oh, right. We should probably wait for the clothes to dry."

Gabe watched while his brother fidgeted. The crackling fire warmed away all of Gabe's shivers. They tried talking to pass the time while their clothes dried, but ran out of words. Finally Gabe grabbed his mostly dry T-shirt and pulled it back on. "I'll show you the tracks."

Ben practically rocketed to his feet, quickly pulling on his own clothes. He carefully put out the fire, then grinned at his brother. "After you."

It didn't take much searching to find the track again. It was still clear in the soft soil. "So, is it a bear?"

Ben shook his head. "That's a cat. A really big cat." He looked up at Gabe and grinned. "The guy at the grocery was right. This is the size of a lion! We might have found the Ozark Howler, little brother!"

chapter 7

Stalked by the Howler

Gabe swallowed and looked around nervously. "We're out here all alone with it."

Ben scratched his head. "I don't know. I can't tell how old this track is. The cat may have been here yesterday. We might be a long way from it, but this is still important evidence."

Gabe could see that idea didn't please his brother, but it made him feel a little better. "Are we going to look for the Howler now?" *Say no, say no, say no,* he thought.

"No," Ben said. "We better follow the creek back to the grocery if we can. Hopefully Ace Rollin isn't filming the Howler right this minute." He turned and began pushing through the brush.

Gabe was happy to follow. Walking was a lot easier with Ben to clear the way. "Orson didn't seem very impressed with Mr. Rollin."

"Orson isn't stupid," Ben said. "Just disloyal."

Gabe didn't know what to say to that, so he just followed his brother. "Sean said the scenic Ozark Mountains are a popular tourist destination. I wouldn't mind running into some tourists right about now."

"That would be great," Ben answered, but Gabe could tell he was barely paying attention, so Gabe stopped talking. It was easier to duck low branches and avoid tripping on roots when he didn't talk anyway. Still, he listened closely for sounds in the woods. He still worried that something had chased that deer into their clearing. Maybe the same something that left the big track.

Unlike Sean, he didn't always like to be right.

As they walked, the dense brush meant they

angled farther from the creek. With the sound of rushing water on their right side, they knew they were headed back toward the grocery and their friends.

The thick brush opened into a long, relatively clear stretch of woods. "Great," Ben said, grinning back at Gabe. "We can pick up some time now."

Before Gabe could answer, a blood-curdling yowl cut through the air behind them. He spun to look, but saw only the thick brush they'd come through.

"Keep walking," Ben said. "Steady, but not too fast."

Gabe swallowed a lump in his throat that blocked whatever he might have said. They both knew better than to run. Running only makes large predators excited. And if there is one thing they didn't want, it was an excited Ozark Howler after them.

They walked quickly across the open land. Ben had fallen back a bit, putting himself between Gabe and the brush behind them. "We should have stayed with the fire," he muttered.

Gabe shot his brother a quick look. "It might not be afraid of fire. I mean, if it was really someone's pet."

"I don't know," Ben answered. "A fear of fire is pretty universal."

Another yowl echoed around them. It definitely sounded closer. The cat was stalking them. Ben pulled his hunting knife out of his pocket and stopped to saw through a sturdy branch.

"Do we have time for that?" Gabe asked. Every nerve in his body was pushing him to run.

"I don't think we have time not to," Ben said. "I need a weapon." He quickly stripped the smaller branches and cut it to about the length of a baseball bat. He swung it a few times, then

turned and handed Gabe the knife. "Here, hold onto this. Don't fall on it."

"I'm not Tyler," Gabe said.

His brother patted him on the back. "I know. Let's keep walking."

It was hard for Gabe to turn his back on the brush behind them, even though they were now almost a third of the way across the long clear area.

Ben stayed right beside Gabe. He never stopped watching the woods around them. Suddenly he stopped.

"What is it?" Gabe asked.

"I'm not sure if we should go on," Ben said. "Once we get back into the brush, our range of vision will be a lot less."

"So you want to stay here?" Gabe asked.

Ben sighed. "If we stay here and it gets dark, we have the same problem, no clear line of sight to see what might be coming at us."

Gabe waited for his brother to decide. Finally he said, "I'm sorry."

"For what?" Ben asked, never pausing in watching the brush.

"I fell in the water and got us in this mess."

Ben shrugged. "If I hadn't brought you guys out here, you wouldn't be in this mess. If Orson hadn't quit my team, you wouldn't be in this mess. There's plenty of blame and none of it useful. What we need now is a plan."

The Howler didn't leave them time for the plan. With another terrifying yowl, something big and black burst from the woods on their left and ran at them.

Frozen with fear, all Gabe could see was teeth and claws and speed.

chapter 8

The Big, Big Cat

Ben met the animal's yowl with a bellow of his own and ran toward it, swinging the heavy branch he'd cut. At Ben's yell and charge, the cat hesitated, then snarled and crouched low to the ground, tail flashing. Ben froze.

Even crouched, the cat was huge. It was as big as a bear, and though it didn't have horns, it looked like the Ozark Howler to Gabe.

Then the late afternoon sun lit the cat's coat. Gabe could see it was covered in dark spots against a charcoal gray fur. He didn't remember spots being part of the Howler description in anything he'd read. What was this thing?

Ben held the branch like a baseball bat and stared down at the cat. "If it attacks me," he said

quietly, "you take off. Get as far away as you can. Understand?"

"Leave you?" Gabe said. "No."

"Don't argue," Ben said, raising his voice slightly. "I promised Mom you'd come home. If it attacks, run."

Gabe looked back at the cat. He could see the muscles bunching under the smooth, spotted skin. The question wasn't if it was going to attack. The question was when.

"Maybe the answer isn't to yell at it," Gabe said. "Maybe it's just scared. Maybe we can calm it down."

Ben shook his head. "No. That's not a risk I'm willing to take."

Gabe eased back toward the brush behind them. "Just try backing away from it, Ben. It can't make things worse. That thing is going to jump at you, soon."

"Fine, but you stay behind me. Way behind

me." Ben took a slow step back away from the cat and so did Gabe. The animal narrowed its eyes, but didn't otherwise move. They continued to back slowly toward the brush. "I'm not leaving the clearing while that thing is here," Ben said. "I don't want it to attack when I don't have room to move and defend us."

Gabe noticed that the cat growled almost every time in response to Ben's voice. Gabe had to admit, it didn't look like it was calming down

much. "I don't think it likes your voice," Gabe said as he eased backward another half step.

"Yeah, well, I'm not thrilled with its growling either," Ben answered. The cat growled again when he spoke.

"Really, you should stop talking." Gabe noticed that the big cat didn't growl when he spoke, though it did look in his direction each time. Ben took another step back toward Gabe, but didn't speak this time.

Gabe began to speak softly, "Nice kitty. Nice kitty." The tail lashing slowed slightly. The cat's eyes stayed on Gabe, even though Ben took another step back. "I think it likes my voice." Ben didn't answer, but he nodded.

Gabe started to take a step toward the cat, but Ben's hand flashed out and grabbed him by the wrist. The cat didn't like the sudden movement. It tensed, then it finally burst forward, running at Ben in terrifying leaps.

Gabe shrieked, nearly drowning out a sharp sound from behind them. Something whooshed by Gabe and buried itself in the big cat's shoulder. The animal yowled and dropped to the ground. It shook its head once, then spun and dashed off into the brush.

A woman wearing a Wild Hope T-shirt and jeans waded quickly out of the brush behind them. She had close cropped black curls and an intense look on her face. Without speaking, she

plunged into the same area of brush where the cat had vanished.

"Who was that?" Gabe asked.

Sean's voice came from behind him, "That was Dr. Rita Iverson. I believe she is waiting for the Howler to pass out. Though I don't think it was still supposed to be able to run after being shot with a knock-out dart."

Gabe grinned at Sean. "You don't know how glad I am to be lectured."

Sean looked at him in surprise. "Then I'm glad to be able to lecture you."

Two more people pushed through the brush behind Sean. Gabe guessed they must have been slowed up by the gear they carried. Tyler struggled under a backpack that bulged at the seams. Orson carried the big camera he'd had in the grocery clearing, as well as a well-stuffed pack of his own.

"I hope you're glad to see us too," Tyler said.

He swung the backpack from his shoulder.

"What's in there?" Gabe asked.

"First aid stuff, clothes, blankets, food," Tyler began ticking things off on his fingers as he recited. "Flashlights, fire starting stuff, water. Water weighs a lot!"

"Got it." Gabe grinned at his friends. "I am so glad to see you guys."

Orson walked up to Ben, tucking the camera under his arm. "How about you? You glad to see me or are you still just mad?"

Gabe listened for his brother's answer.

"Of course I'm glad to see you. That big cat was about to eat us." Ben said. "Besides, I'm not mad at you."

"Yeah, right." Orson looked doubtful.

"I was mad," Ben admitted. "But Gabe made me realize that we've done okay since you left." He shrugged. "Gabe and the guys think outside the box more than the rest of us. It's made a

difference in the show, a good difference."

Gabe felt like his heart was getting warmer in his chest. He had always hoped Ben wasn't too disappointed to work with the Monster Hunters. But hearing his brother talk about it like it was a good thing, well, that was the best kind of shock.

"You know I meant what I said about the show," Orson said. "You're doing good work. Ace is jealous. What we do is fun, don't get me wrong. But you guys are the real deal."

Ben punched his old friend lightly in the arm. "Thanks." He turned to look back at the brush where the woman had vanished. Then he swung Tyler's backpack up onto his shoulder. "But I'm thinking that Dr. Iverson should have come back by now."

"Maybe the Howler is still running," Gabe suggested.

"In that case," Orson said with a grin. "Let's go find a monster."

chapter 9

PROBLEM PET

Gabe and the guys followed Ben and Orson as they plunged into the brush. Shooting a glance at his best friends, Gabe said, "How far are we from the store?"

Tyler groaned. "A zillion miles. We took Dr. Iverson's van down the road for as long as it ran parallel to the river, and we still walked forever to find you."

"As always," Sean said, "Tyler exaggerates. I am certain we walked at least six miles from the spot where we left the van. I should have used my cell phone to measure the distance, but I was distracted by my concern for your well-being."

Gabe grinned and bumped Sean's shoulder. "I missed you guys too."

It took a while to catch up to Dr. Iverson. She stood in a small clearing, frowning as the group joined her. "I've lost its trail."

"How is it still on its feet?" Orson asked. "On TV when something is shot with a dart like that, it falls down right away."

"The load was too small," she said, running her hand across her tight curls in frustration. "I assumed this was an escaped pet. I was expecting to find a mid-sized cat, maybe the size of an ocelot. But that animal is huge. I didn't get a very long look at it, but it's marked like a black jaguar. Still, that's big and heavy, even for a jaguar."

"That's because it's not a pet," Tyler said. "It's the Ozark Howler."

"I am certain that this is the animal causing the Howler reports," she agreed. "In the short look I got, I'd say it weighs over 300 pounds."

"So is it the Ozark Howler?" Ben asked. "Is it

some kind of hybrid of bear and cat?"

She shook her head. "I think we are looking at a mixed animal. But this is all cat, maybe a mix of jaguar and lion. It has the heft of a lion mix."

"Jaguars are native to South America and Mexico," Sean said. "And lions are from Africa. The odds are against a jaguar and a lion having babies in the mountains of Northern Arkansas."

She shook her head. "My guess is that is a cat someone bred intentionally. Collectors pay a lot for mixed-breed exotic pets."

"But that animal is huge!" Tyler said. "No one would want that thing for a pet."

"You'd be amazed," Dr. Iverson said. "Tigers are the largest of the big cats. In the wild, they kill people every year. But my organization estimates there are at least six or seven thousand tigers in the United States and only about 400 of them are in zoos. People think they can raise a tiger cub like a house cat. They're wrong."

Then Orson's cell phone rang and he snatched it out of his pocket. "Mr. Rollin, yep, we found Ben and Gabe. We found the cat too, but it's not the Howler." He explained what Dr. Iverson said. "She is the expert, boss. I think she knows what she saw."

When he finally stuffed the phone back in his pocket, he said, "Ace is on his way out here."

"Goody," Ben replied. "That should make everything better."

"We need to find the cat before they get here," the doctor said.

For the next hour, they slipped through the woods as quietly as they could. They found tracks. Twice they heard the big cat yowl, but the animal seemed to be leading them in circles.

"It's going to be dark soon," Tyler said. "Shouldn't we go back to the hotel?"

The doctor gave him a sharp look. "I'll be staying out here until I find this cat. It's too

dangerous to leave it. But you guys can go back."

"No thanks," Ben said. "We'll stay to the end of the story."

"Me too," Orson chimed in, then grinned when Ben frowned at him. "Besides, I should be here when Rollin shows up."

The doctor stopped and looked around the clear spot where they stood. "With night coming, we should make a camp and build a fire. We'll have to keep watch in shifts since that cat won't be as blind in the dark as we are."

Ben quickly built the fire, and they sat around it, eating. Supper consisted of granola bars, chips, and dried fruit. No one spoke much after the long scary day and the long scary night that stretched ahead of them.

Gabe was sure he'd never fall asleep with the giant cat on the loose, but he soon nodded off. He had no idea how long he'd been sleep when a deep, booming voice woke him up.

"Is this how you earn your keep, Orson?"

Gabe rubbed at his eyes. Ace Rollin stood in one of his action hero poses next to the fire. Orson scrambled to his feet. "Not much else to do since the cat is hiding from us."

"Fire up the camera," Rollin insisted. "This is a great spot to shoot."

"Sure, boss."

As soon as Orson had the camera pointed toward him, Rollin launched into a recap of the hunt for the cat. He got a lot of the facts wrong. He also made it sound like he was there for every step. And he was really loud.

A yowl echoed in the clearing around them. Gabe grabbed his own camera and filmed the bushes, unsure which direction to shoot.

Rollin grinned. "The Ozark Howler is close. You may see the first ever footage . . . " Suddenly, the cat sprang from the bushes and landed within feet of Rollin.

The big man shrieked and jumped back, tripping over one of the rocks that surrounded the fire. On the ground, he kept shrieking as he scooted on his rear away from the cat.

"Everybody stay still," Dr. Iverson said.

Rollin didn't stay still. He kept scooting and shrieking. Gabe kept his camera pointed

at the cat, but he noticed that Orson had his camera pointed at the terrified host on the ground.

The cat shook its head, as if annoyed by Rollin's shrieking. It growled deep and low and took a slow step toward the man on the ground. "Don't just film!" Rollin screamed at Orson. "Save me!"

Orson shrugged but didn't lower the camera. A quick whooshing shot signaled the doctor's rifle and a dart hit the cat in the rump. It spun and snarled in the doctor's direction.

Gabe could see the doctor reloading as fast as she could. He doubted the crouching cat was going to wait for it. But Ben stepped in. He'd picked up his branch from earlier and tossed it at the cat, smacking it in the shoulder. The animal redirected its anger toward Ben, tail lashing.

"No!" Gabe shouted. The cat turned to look at him. Clearly confused about who was the biggest threat. Another shot whooshed, and a dart struck the cat in the foreleg. It yowled and ran for the brush, but two darts were clearly more than it could handle. It managed two bounds, then stumbled and fell nose first to the ground. The encounter was over.

chapter 10

PATCHING UP

"Do you think Rollin will fire you?" Ben asked Orson as they stood in the hotel parking lot.

Orson shrugged. "It's not his call. I got some good footage. Some of it even showed the cat. I think I'm fine."

"Hey," Tyler said. "We finally found out what goes bump in the night."

Orson raised an eyebrow. "What's that?"

"Ace Rollin scooting across the ground!" Tyler laughed wildly at his own joke.

Orson smiled. "I got that on film too. I'm going to suggest the cable company consider a bloopers reel. People love those."

"That will never happen!"

The group turned to see Ace Rollin standing

by the bus. He pointed at Ben. "And I had better not see me on your little web production."

"We're not interested in cable hosts," Ben said. "Just cryptids."

"Though it may be hard to edit all the screaming out of the audio," Sean said.

Rollin made a sound like the Howler growling. He jabbed a finger at Orson. "We're leaving in five minutes, whether you're on the bus or not."

"Sure thing, boss."

Orson reached out a hand to shake with Ben. "It was good to see you."

Ben took his hand, then pulled him in for a hug. "Let's not let so much time pass before we do it again."

"Good plan!" Orson tipped his cap toward Tyler and Sean and thumped Gabe on the back. Then he trotted back to the bus.

"Well, we need to get on the road," Ben said. "Sean, any new cryptid reports?"

Sean pulled out his tablet. "Let me check the message boards."

"Ben, do you think that cat will be all right?" Gabe asked. "It didn't really do anything wrong."

Ben nodded. "Dr. Iverson called this morning. They have a spot for it at Wild Hope. It should be fine."

"I'm glad. And I'm glad you're friends with Orson again."

"Me too," Ben said, throwing an arm around Gabe as they ambled across the parking lot to the van.

Suddenly Sean yelled, "I've got a fresh howler siting!"

Tyler groaned. "I thought we caught that howler!"

Sean grinned. "This one has horns."

Ben whooped and grinned at his team. "Looks like we're monster hunting again!"

Gabe wouldn't have it any other way.